because
of anya

Also by Margaret Peterson Haddix

Among the Betrayed

Takeoffs and Landings

Among the Impostors

The Girl with 500 Middle Names

Turnabout

Just Ella

Among the Hidden

Leaving Fishers

Don't You Dare Read This, Mrs. Dunphrey

Running Out of Time

because of anya

Margaret Peterson Haddix

Aladdin Paperbacks
New York · London · Toronto · Sydney

First Aladdin Paperbacks edition May 2004

Copyright © 2002 by Margaret Peterson Haddix

ALADDIN PAPERBACKS
An imprint of Simon & Schuster
Children's Publishing Division
1230 Avenue of the Americas
New York, NY 10020

Also available in a Simon & Schuster Books for Young Readers
hardcover edition.
Designed by Interrobang Design Studio
The text of this book was set in Janson Text.

Printed in the United States of America
4 6 8 10 9 7 5 3

The Library of Congress has cataloged the hardcover edition as follows:
Haddix, Margaret Peterson.
Because of Anya / by Margaret Peterson Haddix.
p.   cm.
Summary: While ten-year-old Anya faces the difficulties of losing her hair to alopecia, her classmate Keely learns how to stand up for what she knows is right.
ISBN 0-689-83298-2 (hc.)
[1. Baldness—Fiction.   2. Schools—Fiction.]   I. Title.
PZ7.H1164   Ar 2002   [Fic]—dc21
2001057619
ISBN 0-689-86993-2 (Aladdin pbk.)

❧

For Mandy and two Annas

*With thanks to the Doeringer family for sharing
their story with me.*

because of anya

One

The note teetered on the edge of Keely's desk. Quickly Keely swept it into her hand. Then she flinched, waiting for Mrs. Hobson to yell at her.

Mrs. Hobson almost always yelled at Keely when someone passed her a note. Keely wasn't like Tory or Nicole or Stef. The others could flip notes from one side of the room to the other, all day long, and Mrs. Hobson didn't even see. But let one of them pass a note to Keely, or let Keely slide a note under her shoe and inch it toward Nicole's desk, and instantly Mrs. Hobson would boom out in her meanest voice, "Keely Michaels! Do you have something to share with the rest of the class?"

And then Keely would have to beg, "No, Mrs. Hobson. Please, Mrs. Hobson, don't make me read it out loud."

Usually Mrs. Hobson didn't. Usually she just put on her sternest look and pointed at the trash can, and Keely had to walk all the way to the front of the class while everyone else stared at her. Keely always squeezed her eyes shut as much as possible during that long walk to the trash can and back. She couldn't stand seeing the way Tory and Nicole and Stef glared at her.

Once, Stef hadn't spoken to Keely for three days because Keely got caught with a note she was supposed to be passing on to Tory.

Just three weeks ago, right before Christmas break, Stef had announced at recess, "When we come back in January, no one should pass any more notes to Keely. She's going to get the rest of us in trouble."

"But . . . ," Keely had protested. Then she stopped because a little part of her was rejoicing, *That's right! Please don't pass me any more notes! I don't want your notes! They just get* me *in trouble!* But if the others didn't pass notes to her during class, she wouldn't know anything. She'd get to recess and the others would be laughing at jokes she'd never heard, putting the finishing touches on plans that were brand-new to her. "I'll practice," Keely promised. "I'll get better at hiding when you hand me notes."

Stef had narrowed her green eyes, looking straight into Keely's washed-out gray eyes.

"No," she decided. "It's better this way."

And Keely knew that Stef had seen right into Keely's head. Stef knew that Keely knew there was no way she was going to get any better at passing notes.

Keely had worried about that the entire two weeks of Christmas break.

But now it was just the first day back after break, and here was a note, passed straight to Keely, with Keely's name on the outside. Stef was giving her another chance. And—Keely let her shoulders unhunch—Mrs. Hobson wasn't yelling at her for once. Keely didn't look up, but she could hear the scratch of Mrs. Hobson's chalk on the chalkboard. Mrs. Hobson had her back to the class. Keely was safe.

With trembling fingers, Keely slipped the note under her desk and unfolded it. Pretending she was just looking at the bottom edge of her math book, she glanced farther down, at the note.

LOOK AT ANYA!

Even Stef's handwriting was bossy.

Keely looked.

Anya sat at the front of the class, so Keely could barely see anything but the back of her head. Anya wasn't the kind of kid anyone normally paid any attention to. She was just there. She had ordinary brown eyes, ordinary brown hair, ordinary brown clothes. Or maybe not the brown clothes. Keely couldn't remember ever seeing Anya wear anything brown.

But she couldn't even remember what Anya was wearing now, and she'd just looked at her. That's how Anya was. Anya had been in the same class with Keely every year in school—five years altogether now—and Keely probably hadn't really looked at Anya even once since kindergarten.

Keely didn't have the slightest idea why Stef wanted her to look at Anya now.

She glanced over at Stef, three rows away. Stef frowned and mouthed something Keely couldn't understand. Besides not being able to pass notes without getting caught, Keely was also horrible at reading lips.

Stef frowned harder and pantomimed turning over a sheet of paper.

Keely turned the note over in her lap.

I THINK SHE'S WEARING A WIG!!!! Stef had written.

Keely looked at Anya again. A wig? Weird. Keely didn't think she'd ever seen anyone wearing a wig. Certainly not a fourth grader, another ten-year-old like Keely. Keely studied the back of Anya's head. Maybe there was something different about her hair. It was still brown and straight and short, ending right above the collar of her sweatshirt. But it was . . . shinier than usual, wasn't it? And maybe it was thicker. Healthier looking.

Keely glanced back at Stef again, perplexed. Depending on the expression on Stef's face, Keely would know if she was supposed to laugh or be disgusted.

But Stef wasn't looking at Keely. Stef was looking at

Mrs. Hobson, who must have turned around while Keely was staring at Anya.

"Keely?" Mrs. Hobson said. "Do you have something to share with the rest of the class?"

"No, Mrs. Hobson," Keely said. She could feel panicky sweat forming along her hairline. What if this was one of those times when Mrs. Hobson made her read the note out loud? How would Anya feel? Keely could just imagine the embarrassed look on Anya's face, the red blush spreading all the way up to *her* hairline. (To her wig?)

But Mrs. Hobson just pointed at the trash basket. Her knees trembling, Keely got up and started walking.

Two

"You were practically *waving* the note at Mrs. Hobson!" Nicole said as they headed out for recess. "No wonder you got caught!"

"No, I wasn't!" Keely protested. "It was on my lap!"

But had she lifted it up, trying to figure out what Stef was trying to tell her? Tears stung in her eyes, and she angrily blinked them away. She had to be ready. Stef was bound to lecture her again.

But Stef turned around and told Nicole, "Shh. Don't talk about it now. Not until we're . . ." She tilted her head in a signal they all understood. They were going out to the tree to talk.

The tree was *their* spot. It was at the very edge of the playground, past the swings, past the jungle gym, past the baby slides the kindergartners used. It was so far out that sometimes at the beginning of the year the teacher with playground duty had yelled at them, "Hey, where are the four of you going?"

Stef had always gone back to explain. Stef knew how to talk to teachers.

Now they could walk out to the tree and nobody said anything. And nobody followed.

The ground was frozen beneath Keely's feet, but the sun was out and the air was warm. It didn't feel like January. Keely didn't even need her mittens. If Keely hadn't been so stupid as to get caught with that note, she could be enjoying the winter sunshine right now, enjoying being back with her friends, enjoying recess.

They reached the tree. Keely leaned against the bark, letting the tree hold her up.

"Listen," Stef said, lowering her voice even though they were a long, long way from any of the other kids. "Forget about Keely's mistake. Do any of you know *why* Anya's wearing a wig?"

Keely breathed out a silent sigh of relief. She waited for Nicole or Tory to answer. That was how their friendship went. Stef was in charge. She was the one who had decided when they had all gotten too old for dolls. She was the one who had decided soccer wasn't really very much fun after all. She was the one who had decided glitter gel was stupid. She was the one who usually decided what they were going to play every day at recess.

Nicole and Tory were next in line. Sometimes Nicole or Tory could even tell Stef what to do. Just not very often.

And then there was Keely. Sometimes she felt like she was just hanging on by her fingertips. Sometimes it seemed like she was just one mistake away from not having any friends. That's why she tried to keep her mouth shut, whenever possible.

She didn't want to be like Anya. Did Anya ever have anyone to play with?

Nicole shook her blond hair so it bounced against her shoulders. "Maybe Anya thinks she's going to start a new fashion or something," she giggled.

Tory ran her hand through her dark hair. "Well, it's not going to catch on. I'd hate wearing a wig," she said.

Keely noticed that no one waited for her to answer.

"No, no, guys, think," Stef said impatiently. "What if she *has* to wear a wig? Because her own hair is falling out?"

"Eeww," Nicole said, turning up her nose.

"No, listen. What if she has cancer? And her hair's falling out because she has to have chemotherapy?"

Nobody said anything. The tree's empty branches rattled overhead.

Cancer? Keely thought. *Cancer?* She felt like her heart skipped a beat.

"But Anya's just a kid. Like us," Tory said.

"Yeah," Stef whispered. "And she might be dying."

Keely had a sudden memory of kindergarten. The first day, Anya had held the door of the classroom open for Keely to go in in front of her. Keely could remember what Anya had been wearing that day: a frilly pink dress. And Anya's mom or somebody had curled Anya's hair and pulled it back in a big pink bow. Keely had watched those bobbing curls and felt her own fear fade away. Someone was being nice to her already. Maybe school wouldn't be so bad after all.

And now Anya, the first person to be nice to Keely at school, was going to die?

"Somebody would have told us," Nicole said. "Mrs. Hobson or . . . or Mrs. Wiley."

Mrs. Wiley was the guidance counselor. She came into their classroom every month or so and talked about feelings and friendship and having good self-esteem. Stef, Nicole, and Tory always laughed at Mrs. Wiley, but Keely wanted every word she spoke to be true.

"Maybe Anya didn't want anyone to know," Stef said. "Maybe she's being brave and strong, and doesn't want anyone to feel sorry for her. We ought to do something to help her."

Stef got like this sometimes. Just when Keely had decided Stef was the meanest person she knew, Stef would turn everything around and act like the kindest person ever.

Keely could tell that Nicole was feeling bad now for making a face and saying "Eeww" about Anya's hair maybe falling out. Keely herself felt bad for thinking Stef had passed her the note about Anya's wig so Keely would laugh at her.

"What do you think we should do?" Keely asked in a small voice.

"I don't know. . . ." Stef let her voice trail off. She stared off into the distance, watching the other kids on the playground. "There's got to be something we can do to cheer up Anya."

"My mom read this thing in the newspaper," Tory said. "There was this high school football player, see? And he got cancer and had to have whatever that stuff's called—"

"Chemotherapy," Stef said.

"Yeah, that. Anyway, he lost all his hair. And to show how much they cared about him, all the other boys on the football team shaved their heads too. So he wouldn't stand out, because they were all bald."

For one horrible second Keely thought Stef was going to say that was what they'd have to do for Anya. No matter how bad she felt for Anya, Keely didn't want to be bald.

Then she saw Stef's hand fly up to her hair, and Keely knew: Stef would never say they should shave their heads.

Keely had never thought about it much before, but all her friends had really great hair. Tory's was dark and sleek and shiny—it reminded Keely of the seals she'd seen at the zoo, flashing through the water. Nicole's was long and blond, and didn't everyone always want to be blond?

But Stef's was the most impressive of all. It was red and wavy, and stood out like a great cloud around her head. People always noticed Stef, because they noticed her hair.

"Anya would probably just think we were making fun of her if we cut off all our hair," Stef said, like that was the only reason she didn't want to shave her head. "Besides, we don't know that she's bald, just that she's wearing a wig. No, we'll just have to go out of our way to be nice to her. That's what we'll do."

As if Stef had planned it, the recess bell rang just then. All four girls took off running, back to the school. Keely felt her long hair thumping against her shoulders as she ran.

I'm glad I have hair, she thought. *I'm glad I don't have to wear a wig.*

I'm glad I don't have cancer.

Three

Anya pushed open the door. One more step and she'd be inside. Then she could run straight to her room and scratch the place in the middle of her scalp that had been itching all day long. She'd been scared to scratch it, scared she'd knock the wig crooked.

And then everyone would know.

Mom was waiting right inside the front door.

"How'd everything go today?" she asked. Anya heard the strain in Mom's voice, heard how hard Mom was trying to make her words sound like an ordinary question, something an ordinary mom would ask her ordinary daughter on an ordinary day. Anya wanted to say, "Mom, you don't have to pretend too." On an ordinary day Mom would not be perched right on the edge of the living-room chair, waiting to pounce the minute Anya walked in the door.

"Fine," Anya said.

Mom stopped pretending. "Did anybody say anything about your—"

"No," Anya said before Mom had to say that word. *Wig.* "I don't think anybody even noticed."

"Well," Mom said. "That's good, isn't it? So it doesn't matter. We worried for nothing."

Except Anya had wanted to play soccer at recess, but she'd been scared to, for fear of her wig slipping off. And she'd been thirsty after lunch, but she'd been afraid to tilt her head down over the water fountain. And during math she'd dropped her favorite pencil, and rather than bend down to pick it up, she'd watched it roll away. She could imagine the janitor sweeping it up right now.

"I guess," Anya said. But there was tomorrow and the next day and the day after that, all the way up until the end of the school year, and if her real hair didn't start growing back before that—well, Anya still thought she had plenty to worry about. "Hey, you won't believe this. The Staph Infection asked me if I wanted to sit with her on the school bus."

"Anya! You're not supposed to call people names like that!"

Anya just grinned. Staph was a type of bacteria. Anya's

dad knew all about it because he worked in the lab at the hospital. He was the one who'd come up with that nickname for Stef Englewood, the bossiest girl in fourth grade. One night at dinner, when Anya had been telling her parents about Stef trying to make sure she and her friends got the best parts in the class play, Dad had said, "What's that girl's name again? Staph Infection? She sounds pretty lethal to me!"

Mom had said, in that same horrified voice, "Todd! Don't encourage Anya to call people names!" But Anya had loved it. The secret nickname Dad made up seemed to vaccinate Anya once and for all against Stef and the mean things she did.

But that was before.

"So did you?" Mom asked now.

"What?"

"Sit with *Stef* on the bus."

"No. Why would I?" Anya asked.

"To be friends . . ."

"Not with Stef Englewood!" Anya said. She wanted to shake her head for emphasis, but there was the wig to think about.

Secretly she wondered if maybe she would have sat with Stef this afternoon if she hadn't had the wig. But Stef was the kind of person who'd notice.

Heck, she was the kind of person who would reach over and give the wig a tug, just to see if it moved.

"Mom, I have friends," Anya said. "Just not any best, best friends."

"Mmm," Mom said.

Anya knew that if it hadn't been for her hair and the wig, Mom would have said more, would have suggested inviting someone over or signing up for some activity. Mom was the kind of person who liked a lot of people around and something to do every minute.

Anya wasn't like that.

She'd overheard her parents talking about it, plenty of times, when they thought she wasn't listening.

"Maybe we need to force her to get involved with something, take a few chances," Mom always said.

"But as long as she's happy . . . ," Dad always countered.

That was when Anya always stopped listening. Because she had been happy.

Before.

"I think I'm going to go to my room for a while," she told her mother now.

"Don't you want a snack first?" Mom asked.

Anya started to shake her head, then remembered that might not be such a great idea.

"No. I'm not hungry."

"All right," Mom said. But she was biting her lip. Her face was white and strained.

Anya went down the hall, stepped into her room, and shut the door behind her. She slumped with her back against the door, as if she was holding out the rest of the world.

Back when Anya was younger, Mom had turned her room into a pink paradise, with a flowery border stenciled on the walls, a frilly eyelet comforter on the canopy bed, dolls in pink dresses on a shelf above the dresser. Even when she was four, Anya had known the room was more Mom than Anya. Over the years Anya had gradually added a pile of soccer balls and jump ropes in the corner, art supplies spilling across the desk. The pink-dress dolls were long gone, replaced by books about the stars. On her last birthday Anya had begged for, and finally gotten, a new canopy and comforter for her bed—they were the deep blue of the night sky and had tiny pinpricks of silver scattered across them like tiny suns and moons and stars. Looking up into her new canopy every night, Anya could imagine that the roof was gone and she was staring straight up into the heavens. Her room finally felt like it belonged to her.

Except now there was a wig stand smack in the middle of the dresser.

Anya went over to the window and tugged on the shade, making sure it was pulled as low as possible. Then she walked to the dresser.

The wig stand was smooth, rounded plastic, head shaped but blank faced. Anya was glad it didn't have any eyes, a nose, or a mouth drawn on it, like all the stands back at the wig store. She could still feel the way all those eyes had stared at her when Mom said, ever so gently, "You'll have to take your hat off so they can see if the wig fits." Anya knew the eyes were only plastic, only fakes, but it didn't feel that way.

Now Anya reached out and touched the smooth top of her own wig stand. Even without eyes, even without a face, the wig stand seemed to taunt her. "Give me my hair back," the wig stand seemed to be saying. "That's *my* hair you're wearing. You don't have enough hair of your own."

Tears blurred Anya's vision. Forgetting all the instructions for carefully removing her wig, she grabbed the top of it and yanked hard. The toupee tape made a ripping sound letting go. It hurt.

Toupee tape. Anya hated that name. Old men wore toupees. She was a little girl. She shouldn't have to wear anything that had the word *toupee* in it.

Anya tossed the wig, crooked, onto the wig stand. Forget carefully reshaping it. Forget taking good care of it so it'd last a long time.

Then, because she was terrified she might catch a glimpse of herself without the wig, she threw herself across the bed, buried her face in her pillows.

She remembered what Daddy had said: "Hey, it's only hair." He'd been trying to comfort Mom. He wouldn't say anything like that to Anya.

She remembered what the doctor had told her parents: "At least she doesn't have cancer."

Hey, it's only hair, Anya told herself. *At least I don't have cancer.*

But they were only words. They did nothing to loosen the knot of misery in her stomach, nothing to stop the sobs choking out of her throat, nothing to make the hair grow back on her head.

Four

The news threatened to come bursting out of Keely's mouth the minute Mom picked her up from after-school care. But she could tell Mom was too busy barking orders to listen: "Hurry up! We've got to pick up Jacob. The day care called just as I was walking out the door—he's been coughing a lot and they're kind of worried. If he has to stay home sick tomorrow, I don't know *what* I'll do."

What if Anya's cancer had started with coughing? Keely didn't think it worked that way, but still. Jacob was her little brother, just five years old, cute and funny when he wasn't being a pest. Keely almost felt like letting a sentimental tear or two slip out of her eye.

Mom was still talking.

"And Brian's basketball practice ended five minutes ago, and Kevin thinks I'm going to let him have the car tonight to go to play practice. . . ."

Brian and Kevin were Keely's older brothers. They weren't ever cute and funny.

Mom jerked up the door handle of their SUV. She was already reaching for the cell phone before she'd fully slid into her seat.

"Mom, wait," Keely said as soon as she'd scrambled into the back and dumped her book bag on the floor. "I have to tell you something."

"If it's not someone dying, it's going to have to wait," Mom said, still moving fast.

"But it is!" Keely said. "I mean, it might be."

Mom turned around and looked at Keely.

"Anya Seaver has cancer."

"Who?" Mom asked. But her voice was soft now, sympathetic.

"Anya Seaver. She's in my class at school. She's been in my class every year since kindergarten. And now she has cancer."

Mom wasn't turning the key in the ignition. She wasn't reaching for the cell phone anymore. She let out a soft "Ohhh," then was silent and still for a full minute, which was kind of a record for Mom. "What type of cancer does she have? What's the prognosis—oh, I guess that's not something they'd discuss with kids. Oh, her poor parents. I'll have to give them a call and see if there's anything we can do. Is their number in the school directory, do you think?"

"We-e-ell"—Keely twisted uncomfortably in her seat— "I don't think you should call. I think they're trying to keep it secret."

"Then how do you know?" Mom asked.

"Stef said—"

"Oh, *Stef*," Mom said dismissively. She turned the key and began angling out of the parking space.

"No, really," Keely said. She hated it that Mom didn't like Stef. "Stef noticed that Anya was wearing a wig today, and Stef figured out that she must have lost her hair because she's going through chemotherapy, so she must be really, really sick. Only, she must not want people to know."

"Come on, Keely. Are you going to let Stef fool you again?" Mom asked. She was weaving in and out of traffic now. She sped up going through a yellow light on the corner of Hard Road.

"Mom! I saw the wig too!"

Mom was stopped at a red light now. She turned around.

"Keely, *think*. Just because this little girl's wearing a wig, that doesn't mean she has cancer. There could be plenty of other reasons someone might wear a wig."

"Like what?" Keely asked.

"Oh, I don't know," Mom said. "I don't have time to

think about it right now. But I do know that if the girl with the wig—Anya, is it?—isn't talking about it, it's really none of your business. Or Stef's."

The red light turned. Mom hit the gas and sped into the parking lot of Jacob's day care center.

"Just stay in the car," Mom instructed Keely. "I'll be quick. Get some of your homework done while you wait."

Keely watched Mom rush to the door and punch in the code on the security box with lightning speed. Keely could tell: Mom had already forgotten about Anya, already decided there was nothing to worry about, nothing to be done.

Keely wasn't going to forget.

Five

It had started in the fall.

In a way, Anya could see how that might be funny. Leaves let go of tree branches and fell in the fall. Falling stars streaked across the sky in October. Why shouldn't her hair let go of her scalp and fall too?

Mom had noticed it first, one day in November when she was French-braiding Anya's hair before school. Mom had three separate strands of half-braided hair clutched in her left hand, while her right hand gathered the next clump to weave into the braid. Then Mom had suddenly cried out.

"Anya, what is this? You don't have any hair back here!"

"Huh?" Anya said. She'd been reading while Mom braided. She was a million miles away, in Camelot, where Arthur was pulling a sword from a stone.

"Feel back here," Mom said, guiding Anya's fingers to the lower right side of her scalp. "You've got a bald spot the size of a quarter."

The skin was smooth and no hairier than Anya's arm. It didn't even feel like skin that was supposed to have hair growing on it.

"You didn't get bubble gum stuck in your hair and cut it out, did you?" Mom asked.

Anya didn't bother answering such a silly question. She and Mom both knew she wasn't the type of kid to chew bubble gum, let alone get it caught in her hair. And if she'd cut gum out of her hair with scissors, there'd be prickly, shorn hair there now, not blank, smooth skin.

"How long has this been here?" Mom asked.

"I don't know. I didn't know it *was* there," Anya said.

"Well, I'll have to braid your hair differently so that it doesn't show," Mom said. "Maybe I'll call the doctor, too. I've never seen anything like this."

By the time Mom had spoken to the doctor, and he'd referred Anya to a specialist, and she'd finally gotten an appointment to be seen, Anya had two more quarter-size patches of empty skin on her scalp. And any time she brushed her hair, more came out on the bristles.

Anya didn't brush her hair much anymore.

Mom didn't braid it anymore either, because the best style for covering all the bare patches was letting it just hang straight down. Then Anya got a bare spot right on the top of her head.

She had to start parting her hair over on the side and holding it in place over the bare spot with a big silver barrette.

"The doctor will tell us what to do," Mom said as she carefully fixed Anya's hair the Monday before Thanksgiving. "I'm sure we'll have this cleared up in no time."

Anya didn't tell Mom she'd found a fourth spot, just behind her right ear, only that morning. The doctor's appointment was that afternoon. Anya was glad they were finally going to *do* something, and she wouldn't have to have Mom fussing over her hair ever again.

But the doctor didn't smile and give her medicine and tell her she'd soon be cured. He frowned.

"We'll have to do some tests," he said. "But it looks like alopecia areata."

"Alo-what?" Mom said.

Anya thought that whatever alopecia areata was couldn't be too bad, because it was such a pretty name. Alopecia areata shouldn't be a disease or a condition or whatever it was. It should be one of the ladies in King Arthur's court. It should be the name of a foreign beauty queen.

"The best way I can explain it is that she has become allergic to her own hair," the doctor said. "It's an auto-immune disease, though when I say that, people get scared. She's perfectly healthy otherwise. Does anyone else in your family have alopecia areata? There is a genetic compo-nent."

"No," Mom said. "No one. I've never heard of it before."

Anya waited. Any minute the doctor was going to say, "And here's what you do to get your hair back. . . ."

"So, what's the treatment?" Anya's mother asked.

The doctor sighed. "Well, you have some choices. . . ."

Anya let her mind wander while the grown-ups talked about minoxidil and cortisone cream, and which medicines were or were not safe for kids. Anya got bored. There wasn't even anything to look at in the examining room except the doctor's big framed diploma on the wall. Anya read it over three times, even though it was full of words like *henceforth* and *heretofore*. Then she couldn't concentrate on *henceforth*s and *heretofore*s because Mom was getting upset.

"You mean there's a possibility she'll never get her hair back?" Mom was saying. Her voice sounded the way it did when she and Dad were arguing and Mom was about to cry. "And she might lose the rest of her hair too?"

"I didn't say it was *likely*," the doctor said. "But I wanted to prepare you for all the possibilities. Alopecia areata is a very capricious disease. It's impossible to predict what will happen. Some people forego treatment and regain their hair anyway, and never have a repeat episode. Others go through a cycle of losing and gaining for a period of years. Others go completely bald and even lose their eyebrows. Then there's alopecia universalis, where people lose every bit of hair on their entire body. But that's very rare."

The doctor had a soothing voice. It flowed like honey, slow and sweet. But Mom seemed immune to his charm.

"How can we make sure that doesn't happen to Anya?" Mom was asking, horrified.

"You can't," the doctor said.

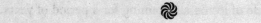

Six

Anya still had her eyebrows. She still had her eyelashes and the tiny, light hair on her arms. But by Christmas she didn't have enough hair on her head to look normal.

"It's a good thing you got out so early in December this year," Mom said. "Nobody noticed at school, did they? Here, let me put some more of this cream on those spots—your hair is bound to grow back by January."

Anya's grandparents lived too far away to visit for Christmas every year, and this was one of the years that nobody in Anya's family was traveling. So all Christmas break Anya sat inside, hiding out, waiting for her hair to grow back.

Christmas morning Anya's dad didn't get his camera out

like usual and take pictures of Anya-beside-the-tree, Anya-with-her-stack-of-presents, Anya-with-the-bows-pulled-off-her-presents-and-stuck-in-her-hair. Anya heard her parents conferring in the kitchen.

"Shouldn't I . . . ," her dad said. Anya couldn't make out his next few words. Then his voice rose in a question, ". . . like normal?"

"Good Lord, no," Mom said.

Anya looked at the tower of wrapped boxes beside the tree. She'd gotten more presents than ever.

She didn't want any of them.

At Christmas dinner she shifted mashed potatoes around her plate with her fork. She stabbed chunks of turkey but didn't bother bringing the forkful up to her mouth. And Mom and Dad, who were usually big promoters of the Clean Plate Club, didn't say a word.

She took to wearing an old baseball cap that had belonged to her dad when he was a boy. It said CINCINNATI REDS across the top. The bill stuck out so far Anya could pull it clear down to her nose, and no one could see her eyes. That was good. Anya could cry under that baseball cap and nobody would know.

Five days before Anya was supposed to go back to school, she heard Mom and Dad talking in the kitchen again.

"I know, but what other choice does she have?" Dad said.

Mom came out of the kitchen. She leaned down low beside the couch, where Anya was sprawled reading about Camelot again. Anya hated Camelot now. She hated King Arthur and Lancelot and, most of all, Queen Guinevere. They all had hair. Queen Guinevere had a lot of it.

"Anya?" Mom said. "Let's go buy you a wig."

Seven

Keely woke up early on the second day of school after Christmas break. The one advantage of being the only girl in the family was that she didn't have to share a room with anyone else, so she could do whatever she wanted in the morning. She hated it at sleepovers when she had to lie there, without moving, and wait until Stef and Tory and Nicole woke up too.

This morning she slipped out of bed and crept over to her desk, where she pulled out her box of crayons and a sheet of clean white paper. She folded the paper in half, like a card, and wrote on the front in her cheeriest purple, GET WELL SOON. Beneath those words she drew a girl in a light blue shirt and darker jeans. The girl even sort of looked like Anya, with brown hair and brown eyes and a shy smile. Keely drew in the bangs carefully, arching them ever so slightly. There were plenty of things Keely couldn't do very well, but even Stef and Tory and Nicole admitted that Keely was the best artist in the class.

Keely finished drawing the girl and flipped the card open. She drew roses and daisies on the inside left page. Now, what should she write on the inside right? She'd already used "Get well soon." Though maybe that wasn't right, because what if Anya wasn't going to get well? What Keely wanted to say was, "I hope you don't die," but that didn't sound like something you should write in a card. It didn't sound like something you should even say. Maybe Anya didn't know that she might die. Keely sure didn't want to be the one to tell her.

After a minute she just wrote, "FROM KEELY."

Keely shut the card and looked at the front again, admiring her drawing of the girl. That was probably the best job Keely had ever done drawing hair.

Oh. Oh, no.

What if it bothered Anya that the picture Keely drew of her had so much hair, when Anya herself had to wear a wig?

What if it bothered Anya that Keely even knew she was sick?

Keely stared at the card for a moment longer. She didn't want to throw it away, because she'd done such a good job on it. And she did want Anya to see it. She did want Anya to know that she, Keely, didn't want Anya to die.

Keely could hear the soft whirring sound coming from Mom and Dad's bedroom, which meant that Mom was awake and already exercising on her treadmill. In a few minutes Mom would burst into the room, tossing off commands: "Get dressed! Go pack your lunch! Go get the Rice Krispies down for Jacob, will you?" And then it'd be breakfast time, and Dad would be passing out good-bye hugs before he rushed off to work, and Kevin and Brian would be joking around, saying, "Hey, Keely! Jacob spit in your juice. Can we watch you drink it?" And Keely wouldn't know if they were telling the truth or not. She'd be so busy guarding her breakfast from her brothers' pranks that she wouldn't have a single moment to think about helping Anya.

Keely slid the card into her backpack to take to school. She could decide what to do with it when she got there.

Maybe Stef would have a good idea.

Eight

It rained, and they had indoor recess on the second day that Anya had to wear her wig to school.

Usually during indoor recess Anya played on the classroom computers with Jennifer and Tyler and Mike, or she played one of the board games with Leah and Kruti, or she drew pictures on the chalkboard with Yolanda and Fumi. But kids were supposed to use headphones with the computers, and Tyler had a bad habit of snatching headphones from other people's heads, without warning, just to be funny. Anya could picture in her mind what would happen if she did the computer: Tyler would grab the top of the headphones, get a handful of Anya's hair caught in his fingers, pull straight up, and suddenly have her whole wig dangling from his hand.

She couldn't play on the computer. The army, navy, air force, and marines combined couldn't get her to touch one of those headphones again until her hair grew back.

But board games were no better. Leah and Kruti always set up their Scrabble or Boggle on the floor, and they bent their heads in together, spelling words. How could Anya be sure Leah or Kruti wouldn't lean too close, get a good look at Anya, and call out in horror, "Is that a wig?"

Or—Kruti wore earrings. Anya could even imagine one of Kruti's earrings getting caught in Anya's wig, pulling it sideways. Kruti would scream. Everyone would hear.

No board games.

But drawing on the chalkboard wasn't a great idea either. Fumi and Yolanda liked to lean way back and draw their pictures up to the very top of the board. If Anya leaned way back, she might not still have a wig on when she straightened up.

Anya couldn't do anything.

When first recess came, Anya sat frozen at her desk, watching the other kids scatter around the room. But then she really stuck out, the only one still left in her seat. Any minute Mrs. Hobson might look up from the papers she was grading and say, "Anya? Didn't you hear? It's recess. Are you all right, dear?"

Anya slipped a book out of her desk and went to a corner

away from everyone else. She hunched over in as small a space as possible and started reading.

It was the Camelot book again.

Anya could have chosen any one of a dozen other books to read. Mrs. Hobson was big on encouraging kids to read; two whole shelves full of paperbacks lined the wall under the windows. Mrs. Hobson would probably have even let Anya go down to the school library to get a new book, if she had asked.

But Anya had been reading the Camelot book when she found out about her first bald spot. She'd been reading the Camelot book when Mom told her she was getting a wig. It didn't seem like she'd be able to move on to anything else until her hair grew back.

She knew what the books on Mrs. Hobson's shelves were about. Half of them told about kids who had really stupid problems, like they wanted a dog and their parents wouldn't let them have one. And they thought that was the greatest tragedy in the world. Anya just couldn't care anymore about kids like that.

The other half of the books were about kids who had really, really awful things happen to them, like their best friend died, or they were in a car wreck and lost their legs, or they had bad parents who beat them up all the time. That kind of book would make Anya even sadder than she already was.

So she was stuck with Camelot. Morgan le Fay was just about to betray Arthur.

Anya read in the corner for the whole recess. Nobody

came over and said, "Oh, Anya, we were waiting for you. Come on, play with us." When Mrs. Hobson called everyone back to their desks, no one leaned across the aisle to say—fast, before Mrs. Hobson started in on science— "Hey, Anya, I know you did something else this recess, but will you play with us next recess?"

It had never mattered before that Anya played with some kids some of the time, other kids other times. Anya had always liked that, before. Some days she felt like listening to Tyler's goofy jokes and Jennifer's rowdy riddles; some days she liked the peaceful swoop of the chalk on the board beside easygoing Fumi and quiet Yolanda.

But going back and forth between friends meant that no one missed her, no one wondered where she was. Nobody knew how awful she felt—how, even now, even as Mrs. Hobson talked about photosynthesis in her calm, patient voice, Anya's stomach was churning and she kept having to squinch her eyes together to make sure there weren't any tears forming and falling. Nobody knew how scared she was that her wig might be even the teeniest bit crooked. Nobody saw how she kept having to lift her hand toward the wig, to feel the tips of the fake hair, to make sure nothing was wrong.

But she didn't want anyone to see. She didn't want anyone to know.

Did she?

Nine

All recess Keely and her friends whispered together. Keely missed their tree outside. At the tree everyone talked out loud, and Keely could hear well. Inside, no matter how close Keely tried to sit, she always missed something.

They were talking about Anya.

"Well, I think we should tell her we know," Tory said.

"Shh," Stef said. "I'm thinking."

Keely turned and looked over her shoulder. Anya was in the opposite corner, bent over a book. She was the only kid in the whole room sitting alone. Keely couldn't see her face. Between the book and the hair falling forward to hide her eyes, Anya might as well have been behind a curtain.

"I made a card for Anya," Keely said. "I'm going to give it to her."

"No!" Stef said. "I mean, let's take this slow, make sure we're doing the right thing."

This wasn't like Stef. Stef usually charged ahead, no matter what. She was always sure she was doing the right thing.

Was Stef scared? Stef?

"All right, class, back to your seats. Recess is over," Mrs. Hobson said.

Keely sat through science, barely listening to Mrs. Hobson talking about how plants got food and survived. Too much else was whirling around in her brain. She stared at the glossy hair on the back of Anya's head.

Back in kindergarten Keely and Anya had been friends. Kind of. Almost. Keely could remember those first few weeks of school. During free choice she and Anya were the only two girls who wanted to play with the blocks. It seemed like all the other girls rushed straight to house-keeping—the toy kitchen and the three-legged table with the plastic fruits and vegetables. But Anya and Keely had built towers together. Keely thought she had even asked Mom once if Anya could come over to play at her house, but Mom had said no. Jacob was born when Keely was in kindergarten. Mom said no a lot that year.

And then in the second month of kindergarten Stef had moved into the class. She'd latched on to Keely right away.

(Why hadn't she latched on to Anya?) Stef told Keely that blocks were boring. She liked to play at the art table. And Keely did too. Stef told her what to draw, and then Stef would glue Keely's pictures onto mobiles and collages, or cards that Stef took home and gave to her own parents.

Keely couldn't remember anything else about Anya from kindergarten. Once Stef arrived, it was like she was the star of the show, and Keely's memory didn't have room for any of the bit players. Stef invited Keely over to her house plenty of times. Stef nagged and nagged Keely, so Keely finally talked Mom into letting her have Stef over.

Now Keely could picture Anya, five years old, in pink overalls, standing beside a block tower waiting for Keely. And Keely never came, because she was off playing with Stef.

But that was silly. Keely could play with anyone Keely wanted to. Anya could play with anyone Anya wanted to. All that had been four and a half years ago. It didn't matter now. It didn't have anything to do with Anya wearing a wig, and maybe having cancer, and maybe dying.

Did it?

At the next recess Stef gathered her friends together, leaned forward, and announced dramatically, "I have a plan."

Ten

Anya was hunched over her Camelot book again at second recess. It was a good thing this was the fourth time she'd read this book, because she wasn't absorbing any of it. She'd read a sentence, get to the period at the end, and realize she couldn't remember a single word.

"Hi, Anya," someone said.

Anya jerked her head up. Automatically she reached her hand up to feel the wig, to make sure she hadn't knocked it crooked.

Keely Michaels was crouching beside her.

"Hi," Anya said. Her voice came out almost like a croak. It seemed like days since she'd used her voice.

Never mind that she'd answered a math question for Mrs. Hobson just ten minutes earlier. Anya felt like she was some hermit who'd been living in a cave for decades, and she didn't know what to do when someone showed up to talk to her.

Instinctively Anya scooted away from Keely so that she couldn't get a close look at the wig.

"I just came over to tell you," Keely said, "um, your hair looks really good today. Did you just get it cut?"

"Uh, yeah. Over the holidays." Anya's voice came out in a terrified whisper. The thing was, she wasn't lying. The wig shop had cut and shaped the wig to fit her head before she took it home.

"Where?" Keely persisted.

"What?" Anya said.

"Where did you get your hair cut?"

Anya shrugged. "Just some hair place. I don't remember the name."

Now, that was a lie. Anya would never forget Josephine's Wig Shop. Even if she lived to be a million years old, even if her hair grew back tomorrow and never fell out again (oh, please, God, let her hair grow back tomorrow and never fall out again), she'd still have nightmares about Josephine's Wig Shop. Everybody had been nice to her, but that only made it worse. At the end, when the wig was all cut and shaped and stuck tight on Anya's head, three workers had clustered around her, exclaiming, "Oh, don't you look nice," and, "No one would ever know," and, to Mom, "You have such a beautiful little girl."

None of the workers were wearing wigs.

But a practically bald old woman sat in the try-on chair beside Anya's. She had hollow cheeks and sunken eyes; she looked barely alive. The dark wig the workers were placing on her bare head only made the woman's face look more cavernous. Anya was sure the woman was really, really sick. And she was the only one in the store not telling Anya how pretty she looked. She didn't say anything. But the old woman's eyes met Anya's in the mirror, and that exchanged glance was the only thing that gave Anya the courage to stand up and walk out of the store.

The old woman understood. She understood that Anya didn't feel pretty or nice. She understood that what Anya wanted to do was yank the wig off her head and throw it on the ground and scream, "Quit lying to me! Leave me alone! Take that horrid thing away! I hate it! I hate you all!"

Because the old woman wanted to do the same thing.

"Um, are you feeling okay?" Keely asked now.

"Yeah," Anya said. "Why?"

"I just wondered," Keely said. "You, um, look a little pale. You're not getting sick, are you?"

"No," Anya said. "I'm fine. Never felt better."

She could practically see the lies piling up, like they were something tangible. Bricks being laid on mortar, maybe.

Tell enough lies and she wouldn't need the wig anymore, she'd have a whole wall built around her.

"Oh," Keely said. "Great. I'm glad."

Anya didn't say anything.

"Well, I've got to go," Keely said, like she had an important appointment she couldn't miss. "It's been nice talking to you. See you later."

Anya watched over the top of her book as Keely scurried across the room, back to Stef Englewood and the rest of her little clique.

What had that whole conversation been about?

Anya realized she was sweating; her heart was beating so hard it felt like it was trying to escape. Cautiously she rubbed her hand across her sweaty forehead. Sweat didn't look very natural on synthetic hair.

Across the room she could see Keely talking animatedly with her friends. Keely was shaking her head. Her voice rose, loud enough that Anya could catch three short words: "No, I couldn't . . ."

And Anya told another lie, just to herself: *They're not talking about me.*

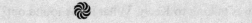

Eleven

"**M**aybe you should just tell," Dad said.

"Huh?" Anya and Mom said together.

They were eating dinner, enchiladas, which were usually one of Anya's favorite meals. But the food seemed strangely tasteless tonight. Something had made Anya open her mouth and start telling Mom and Dad about Keely coming over and complimenting her hair. Anya had wanted to make the story something good—she'd wanted to finish with the words, "So, see? Nobody notices a thing! They think I just got a haircut and it looks great." Anya had wanted to erase the worry she saw in her parents' eyes.

But the story had come out all wrong. Anya had even found herself saying, "I was just so scared the whole time I was talking to Keely. What if she found out?"

When Anya was done talking, Mom and Dad looked even more worried. They exchanged glances, and then Dad burst out with his, "Maybe you should just tell."

"What good would that do?" Mom said after she and Anya got over their shock. "That would just make sure that the thing she's scared of would happen. Pretty soon everybody would know."

"Exactly," Dad said. "She shouldn't tell just this Keely kid. She should tell everybody. What if she stood up in front of her class and said, 'Listen up, everyone. Something weird happened to me over Christmas break. My hair fell out, and now I'm wearing a wig. But it's no big deal. What I have isn't contagious and it doesn't hurt and I'm perfectly healthy otherwise'? Then everybody would know, and she wouldn't have to be scared anymore."

"People would ask questions," Mom said.

"So what?" Dad said. "Anya could answer them."

Tears stung in Anya's eyes. Dad thought she was brave enough to tell, but she wasn't. There was no way she could do what Dad was suggesting. She didn't even want to think about it.

Dad put his fork down.

"As much as I hate to think it, this alopecia is probably something we're going to have to deal with for a long time.

Maybe we even have to acknowledge that Anya may never get her hair back."

No, Anya thought. *No.*

Dad wasn't done talking.

"And I think the only way we can survive it is to be honest about it. I'm willing to go first." He turned and looked directly at Anya. "Anya, ever since you lost that first patch of hair, I've been beating myself up, thinking it's my fault somehow. What if it's connected to some germ I brought home from the hospital? What if it's because of some genetic defect that you inherited from me? I've been working in some field of medicine since I was eighteen years old—why can't I just do a little research and pull some obscure cure off the Internet and make it all better for you?"

"Todd, you can't be so hard on yourself," Mom said. "None of this is your fault."

"I know," Dad said. "And it's not your fault, and it's certainly not Anya's fault. It's just something that happened. And it may end, and it may not, and we've just got to go on with our lives regardless."

"Daddy . . . ," Anya said, and couldn't go on. Her face twisted. Why did her body keep betraying her? First her hair fell out, now she couldn't keep from crying. Rather than sit there sobbing in front of Mom and Dad, she whirled around and raced to her room.

Anya buried her face in her pillow. Then she yanked

another pillow over the rest of her head. She didn't care how badly she mashed her wig. Yes, she did—she stopped crying long enough to jerk the wig from her head and fling it to the floor.

Someone knocked at her door.

"Anya?" Mom called. "Can I come in?"

"I just want to be alone right now," Anya called back. She sniffed. "I'm sorry I didn't ask to be excused."

Anya expected Mom to come in anyway and sit on the side of the bed and stroke Anya's hair—no, pat her back, maybe—and tell Anya she shouldn't cry, everything was going to be all right. But Mom didn't. Anya heard the footsteps that meant Mom was walking away.

That made Anya cry even harder.

Anya didn't know how long she cried, but she soaked both pillows with tears and used up half a box of Kleenex wiping her eyes and nose. When she couldn't cry anymore, she sat up dizzily. The room was dark. For all she knew, it could be the middle of the night. No—Mom and Dad were still up. Anya could see a thin line of light under the door and hear the hum of voices that meant they were sitting in the living room talking.

Anya was thirsty. It seemed like she'd used up every last drop of liquid in her whole body making tears. Shakily she slipped out of bed. The crying had made her lightheaded and weak-kneed; she felt like some invalid who'd been confined to her bed for months.

But she'd felt like an invalid even before she started crying. It was like she wasn't even herself anymore, Anya Seaver. She was someone else, some disabled person who couldn't even grow hair.

You're thirsty, Anya reminded herself, before she started crying again. *Go get a drink.*

Anya bent over and placed the wig back on her head. Then she pushed open her door and stepped into the dim hall. She turned toward the bathroom. She could hear Mom and Dad better now, but she didn't feel like talking to them yet. She was glad of the wall that shielded her from them.

Then she heard what they were saying.

"No, I can't cope with this!" Mom was sobbing. "This is my little girl! I keep looking ahead—what's it going to be like for her when it's summer and all the other kids want to go to the swimming pool but she can't? What's it going to be like when she gets to middle school and they have sleepovers where they do each other's makeup and hair? What's it going to be like when she gets to high school and nobody wants to date her because she's bald?"

Anya couldn't hear Dad's answer. She couldn't make herself keep walking toward the bathroom, either.

"And you wonder why I don't think we should keep trying for another baby?" Mom cried. "Maybe put another child through this agony?"

Anya froze, as still as if she'd been turned to stone. She

couldn't have moved if she'd wanted to. *Not that*, she thought. *Alopecia's not going to take that away too*.

Anya remembered a perfect day last September when she and Mom and Dad had taken a picnic to the state park. All three of them had thrown a Frisbee back and forth; Dad got the soccer ball out, and they played a crazy game where Anya got to be goalie for both teams. It ended when all three collapsed in a heap together, laughing.

"Anya, you really need a brother or a sister to help you defend those goals," Dad had said.

And Anya had looked from Dad to Mom, and she'd seen that it wasn't a joke. And then both Mom and Dad had explained that they were thinking about having another baby, and they weren't sure how Anya would take the news, because she'd be so much older than her brother or sister, but—

"Are you kidding?" Anya had interrupted. "I'm thrilled! I'm delighted! I'm"—she came up with one of Mrs. Hobson's vocabulary words—"ecstatic!"

She was so overjoyed she'd done cartwheels, right there in the grass, six or seven in a row.

That was when she could still do cartwheels without worrying about her wig falling off.

For weeks after that picnic Anya had imagined a new baby in the family. She had imagined the baby clapping her little hands, cooing and gurgling with joy when Anya got home from school. She had even imagined taking the baby for walks in a stroller, to give Mom a rest, and having all the neighbors stop and admire the baby and tell Anya, "Well, aren't you a good big sister."

Those daydreams hadn't exactly fallen out of her head along with her hair. She'd just pushed them to the back of her mind, to wait in suspended animation until her hair grew back.

And now Mom was saying she didn't want a baby anymore, because of the alopecia.

Because of Anya.

Anya turned and fled back to her room to cry some more.

Twelve

Keely had stood up to Stef.

Keely lay in bed that night, practically hugging herself with joy and wonderment and—yes—relief. She'd stood up to Stef and nothing had happened.

Keely never stood up to anybody. She'd never stood up to her brothers when they teased her. She'd never stood up to Mom when Mom was rushing around tossing off orders like a drill sergeant. And most of all, Keely had never stood up to Stef or Tory or Nicole.

But that afternoon Keely had.

Keely propped herself up on one elbow and stared out

the window at the full moon while she relived the end of second recess in her mind.

Talking to Anya had been . . . hard. Anya just had such a miserable look in her eyes. Keely had never seen someone so sad. She *ached* for Anya. And the longer Keely talked to her, the more certain Keely was that she wouldn't do what Stef wanted her to do: tug on Anya's wig and see if it moved.

"Well, I've got to go," Keely had finished up. "It's been nice talking to you. See you later." Keely's hands didn't move up toward Anya's wig; she didn't even lean in close to try to see what was under the wig. Then she walked back to where Stef and Tory and Nicole were waiting. She felt like a hero returning from war—a hero like Martin Luther King or Gandhi, because she'd refused to fight, refused to do anything cruel.

"You could have just given her hair a little pull," Stef said when Keely reported the entire conversation and admitted what she hadn't done.

"No, I couldn't," Keely said. "You weren't *there*. You didn't see the look on her face. Stef, I think she really is dying. I'm not going to do something mean like that to someone who's dying."

And it was Stef who dropped her eyes, Stef who couldn't meet Keely's gaze, Stef who was ashamed.

"Then one of you do it," Stef said to Tory and Nicole.

Slowly, very slowly, Tory and Nicole shook their heads, declining.

They were more scared of Anya than they were of Stef. They didn't even want to go near someone who might be dying. They weren't as brave as Keely.

Stef's face turned red then, and her eyes got hard. This was a look that Keely had always been terrified of before. Before, that look would always send Keely scrambling to do whatever Stef wanted—telling Kruti her earrings were ugly, telling the third graders they weren't allowed to sit at Stef's table during lunch, telling Mom that Keely absolutely, positively had to have a Limited Too shirt like everyone else. All those things that made Keely's stomach churn and her skin crawl. She didn't like Limited Too shirts. She hated being mean. She just hated even worse to have Stef mad at her.

But at second recess Stef's angry look didn't transform Keely into an obedient slave, as usual. At second recess Keely narrowed her own eyes, glared right back at Stef.

"And Stef, so help me, if you pull Anya's hair yourself, I'll never speak to you again."

Thirteen

The third day that Anya had to wear her wig to school was gym day.

The gym teacher, Mrs. Vance, had announced back in December that as soon as they came back from Christmas break, they'd be starting gymnastics.

Gymnastics. Somersaults. Cartwheels. Handstands. Backbends. Flips.

Anya didn't even like leaning over, for fear of losing her wig. With gymnastics, Mrs. Vance might as well have been plotting to humiliate Anya.

The ladies back at Josephine's Wig Shop had given her a few tips for dealing with phys ed.

"Your wig will stay on and be secure under normal circumstances," the tallest woman—Josephine?—had said. "But a lot of our girls have found that it's a good idea to wear a headband when you have gym."

"Oh," Anya had said weakly.

Nobody wore headbands at school. Headbands hadn't been in style since second grade, when Stef Englewood and her friends all decided to grow out their bangs at the same time, and they needed some way to keep all the in-between-length hair out of their eyes. Anya had kept her bangs. She didn't even own one of those stupid little plastic headbands.

But the headband Josephine was talking about wasn't little and plastic. It was elastic and wide—at least two inches across—and it circled Anya's entire head.

"There!" Mom said as she finished helping Anya put her wig on the morning of gym day. She snapped the headband in place. "What do you think?"

Mom was being extra cheerful this morning. Unless you looked really closely at the puffiness around her eyes, you'd never know she'd been sobbing her heart out on Daddy's shoulder the night before.

Anya tried not to look really closely. She didn't look in the mirror Mom was holding out either.

"Feels tight," Anya said. She gave her head an experimental shake. The wig didn't budge. "I don't think it'll fall off."

"The headband's kind of cute, too," Mom said. "I predict everyone will be asking where you got it."

Then what will I say? Anya wondered. *"Josephine's Wig Shop"? "Shave your head and go down there right now"?*

But Mom's perkiness tricked her into looking in the mirror. Anya was almost surprised to see her own familiar face staring back at her: the familiar brown eyes, the thin nose, the lips that were pretending to smile for Mom. Anya felt like she didn't have a right to that face anymore; she felt like such a different person that nobody else should be able to recognize her either.

Above her face the wig was stiff, but cut and tinted to look just like her original hair. In fact, the only thing that looked weird was the headband.

But it looked really, really weird. It looked like something an old lady would wear—and not a normal old lady either. It'd have to be some old lady who still wore the same clothes she'd worn back in the 1960s: gaudy calf-length pants in unnatural colors like neon lime and electric orange, wild shirts with huge flowers or geometric designs. And, to top it all off, some thick, bright red headband like Anya's.

"Anya?" Mom said. "Is something wrong?"

I can't go to school looking like this, Anya thought. *Everyone's going to laugh.*

"No," Anya said. "I'm fine."

Fourteen

Nobody laughed. Some people stared—Anya even felt Mrs. Hobson's eyes lingering on her too long during spelling. Stef Englewood and her little gang kept whispering together, and turning around and looking, then whispering some more.

Anya spent as much time as possible during recess hiding out in the bathroom so no one would try to talk to her.

Then it was time for gym.

Anya walked down the hall on shaking legs. This was worse than going to the dentist, worse than going to the doctor to get a shot, worse than that time back in third grade when she'd had to stand up in front of the whole class and give a five-minute speech. It seemed just plain wrong to keep going forward when she knew that what waited for her in the gym might be her worst nightmare.

"Hello, fourth grade," Mrs. Vance boomed as soon as Anya's class stepped into the room. "Ready for some fun?"

Mrs. Vance was the kind of gym teacher who must have hated school when she was a kid herself. She acted like everyone ought to be really grateful to her because phys ed had to be the only enjoyable part of the school day.

"I know you all spent your whole Christmas break wishing and wishing for school to start again so we could get going on the gymnastics unit," Mrs. Vance said. "Well, the moment you've been longing for is finally here!"

She started dividing them up into groups. Anya was hoping for the balance beam, but Mrs. Vance sent Yolanda, Leah, Sammy, and Ryan in that direction. Anya waited, her heart sinking further with every assignment Mrs. Vance doled out.

When just six kids were left, Mrs. Vance announced, "Okay, the rest of you can go practice front and back rolls and cartwheels on those mats over there. We'll rotate you onto the other equipment as soon as possible."

Anya was one of the six kids.

So was Stef Englewood.

Anya stood as far back in the group as possible while

Tyler showed off a dramatically flawed cartwheel.

"Don't you know you're supposed to keep your legs straight?" Stef said. She did a cartwheel of her own, smooth and polished. "I've been taking gymnastics since I was three. This is *so* easy."

Anya didn't pay attention to how straight Stef kept her legs. Anya was too busy watching the way Stef's hair floated around her head—bouncing, then flattening with Stef's leap, flowing toward the ground when she was upside down, settling lightly on her shoulders when she was done.

"All right, Anya, let's see yours," Mrs. Vance said, coming up behind their group.

"M-me?" Anya said.

"Unless you've changed your name," Mrs. Vance said. "See anyone else around here named Anya?"

Anya stepped up to the mat. Why hadn't she gotten Mom to write a note to get her out of gym?

She knew why. If Mom had written a note, she would have had to explain why Anya couldn't do cartwheels or headstands. She would have had to tell Mrs. Vance or Mrs. Hobson or the principal or someone that Anya had lost her hair and was wearing a wig.

Anya raised her hands over her head. She started running, but not too fast. She sprang up but didn't launch her body forward with nearly enough force. She'd barely placed her right hand on the ground before her feet came crashing down. It was the worst cartwheel she'd ever done.

But—she checked quickly—her wig had stayed in place.

"I did better cartwheels than that when I was two," Stef snorted.

"Try it again," Mrs. Vance said, looking at Anya a little strangely. Anya was usually great at phys ed.

This time Anya ran a little faster, leaped a little higher. She actually felt the air whizzing past her face. Somehow she managed to abandon herself to the joy of the cartwheel. She'd show Stef. She could do great cartwheels, even with a wig on.

Anya rose up at the end, triumphant. She stood still, panting.

"Very good," Mrs. Vance said, and moved on to the next group.

Anya's wig had stayed on. It wasn't even crooked.

After that Anya did a roundoff. She stood on her hands and her head. She walked across the balance beam. She felt so free. Her wig didn't move an inch. Maybe she'd just wear a headband every day. She didn't care how weird she looked.

Then, right at the end of phys ed, when her group had rotated back to the mats, she got brave enough to try somersaults.

"How many can you do in a row?" Tyler asked.

"Five," Anya said. "Five between here and the end of the mat."

She bent down and rolled forward, tucking her knees

against her chest. She concentrated on pushing off with her legs, keeping her body in one tight ball. She didn't think about the wig at all.

Roll—roll—roll—roll . . . She was getting dizzy, but she hadn't reached the end of the mat yet. Out of the corner of her eye she could see the other kids in her group stepping forward to see if she could squeeze in the final somersault. Then in the middle of the fifth somersault, as she put the top of her head against the mat, something pulled at her scalp.

Automatically Anya's legs kept pushing, her hands kept shoving off against the mat. Her mind didn't have time to stop the momentum of her body. But her somersault went crooked. She scrambled to her feet. She looked up at the other kids in her group.

All five of them were staring at her, bug-eyed.

"You lost your hair!" Tyler gasped.

It seemed like the whole gym went dead silent after that. The gym was never silent. It was the kind of place where kids screamed at the top of their lungs, and so did Mrs. Vance. But now Anya could practically hear herself blinking. She could feel every single person freeze, staring at her.

Desperately Anya reached up for her wig, wanting to believe that Tyler just meant one hair, or one little strand, was caught on the mat. But Anya's hand went all the way up to the top of her right ear without encountering a single synthetic hair. She didn't let herself reach any higher. She whirled around and saw the wig and the worthless red headband still lying on the mat.

"It's . . ." Anya choked. She felt all those eyes staring at her. She snatched up the wig from the mat and took off running.

Fifteen

Keely was wobbling her way across the balance beam when it happened. One minute she was trying not to fall, the next minute the gym was filled with such an unearthly silence that she had to look up. It seemed like her head automatically jerked in the same direction as everyone else's.

Keely's eyes took in the sight of Anya standing there, wigless, stunned, her mouth agape, her eyes filled with crazy panic. And behind Anya, Stef was snickering silently, her hand cupped over her mouth.

Stef. Stef had pulled off Anya's wig.

Keely was suddenly filled with such fury that she fell off

the balance beam. Nobody seemed to notice because everyone was watching Anya. Besides Keely, Anya was the only one who wasn't frozen in place. Anya had the wig in her hand; she was streaking out of the gym like her life depended on getting away.

The doors slammed shut behind her, and still nobody moved.

Finally Mrs. Vance said, "Children, I believe you should go back to your classroom now."

Mrs. Vance sounded puzzled, like she didn't have the slightest idea what she'd just witnessed. But her voice broke the spell everyone was under. Kids jumped off whatever apparatus they were working on. They all began talking at once.

"Did you see—"

"Why—"

"What's wrong with her?"

"She has cancer," Keely said softly. Then she spoke louder. "She has cancer and she's really sick and she might even die. And Stef just pulled her wig off."

The buzz of voices grew as Keely's news crossed the room. Keely closed her eyes, weakly. She could make out just one word in all the buzzing.

"Stef . . ."

"Stef . . ."

"Stef . . ."

Sixteen

The classroom, the bathroom, the janitor's closet . . .

As she ran Anya kept thinking of—and then rejecting—places to hide. She zigzagged down the hall, veering away from doors with every idea she discarded. There was no place to hide at school, no place she could be sure she wouldn't be found.

She crammed the wig onto her head, holding it in place with her left hand while she shoved open the door to the playground with her right. She kept waiting for someone to stop her, but nobody did. The playground was empty. The parking lot beyond was full of cars and nothing else.

Anya kept running. As long as her legs kept pumping, she didn't have to think, didn't have to remember the sight of all those shocked faces, all staring at her exposed head.

Anya was off the school grounds now. She was into the neighborhood behind the school. She'd never done anything like this before. She'd never skipped school, never run away. She'd always been a good kid, sitting in her seat, never even making a peep unless the teacher gave her permission.

But she'd never had her hair fall out before. She'd never lost her wig in the gym before and had twenty-two kids staring at her bald head.

Anya ran faster. The only place she could think to go was home, and that was a mile away. She'd never run that distance before, never even walked it, but she knew she could get there today. She had to.

By the time she reached her family's own familiar picket fence, she was panting in great, huge gulps that might be considered sobs if she let herself think about it. She had a stitch in her side and her legs were shaky, but she unhooked the latch and stepped into her own yard. She pulled up the rock in the front flower bed that had the key hidden underneath, and let herself into the house.

The house was empty—both Mom and Dad were at work—but Anya still didn't feel safe enough. She dragged herself into her own room. The wig stand was still on her dresser, so she threw it out into the hall. She threw the wig after it. She locked her door and propped her chair against the knob. Then she crawled into bed.

It didn't seem like enough to be under the comforter, so she burrowed under the blankets and the sheets, even the bottom one. She lay with her cheek against the rough weave of the mattress and sobbed and sobbed and sobbed.

In no time at all, it seemed, Mom was there—no, Mom and Dad both, both crying and calling out, "Oh, honey . . . ," "Oh, Anya . . ." Anya didn't even think to wonder how they'd found her, how they'd gotten in through the locked door and the propped chair, how they'd known to leave work and come to her. She let Mom cradle her in her arms like a little baby. She let Daddy's tears fall on her own bare scalp.

"They *saw*," Anya kept crying. "They know. Everyone knows."

She pushed herself away from Mom's hug; she brushed away the tears that could have been Daddy's or Mom's or her own.

"I'm never going back to school again," she said. "Please. Don't make me. I won't go."

Seventeen

Mrs. Hobson gave everybody math sheets to work on, but even Yolanda, the smartest kid in the class, couldn't seem to make herself push her pencil across the paper, marking down meaningless answers. Whispers floated across the classroom, but Mrs. Hobson didn't yell at anyone to shut up.

The classroom phone rang. Mrs. Hobson sprang toward it.

"Yes? Yes, I see. Mm-hm. Well, that's good, at least. Is it—"

Mrs. Hobson was silent, listening, for a very long time.

"Oh," she said finally. "Yes, we will." She hung up.

Keely raised her hand.

"Is Anya going to die?" she asked.

"Anya doesn't have cancer," Mrs. Hobson said. "I don't know where that rumor came from."

"Then what does she have?" Tyler spoke up. "You didn't see her, Mrs. Hobson. If you had, even you'd be saying, 'Dude, that ain't normal.'"

"Tyler," Mrs. Hobson said warningly. "You're talking about a fellow member of this class, a fellow human being, someone who is now telling her parents she never wants to come back to school because you all saw her without her wig."

Mrs. Hobson paused long enough to let that sink in. Keely took the time to glare over at Stef.

"I didn't know this myself," Mrs. Hobson finally continued, "but Anya evidently has a disease called alopecia areata—a-lo-pee-she-uh air-e-ah-ta—I think I'm saying that right. Her father told me she just began showing signs of it in the fall, but the disease progressed rapidly in December. So she's been wearing a wig since we came back from Christmas break. Anya's been very embarrassed about it and didn't want anyone to know. Her dad says alopecia areata is not painful and not deadly and not contagious."

Tory, who'd been waving her hand in the air, abruptly put it down.

Mrs. Hobson sank back into the chair behind her desk.

"I must say, this is a difficult situation to deal with," she continued. "It's unfortunate what happened during gym. Not just that you all saw Anya without her wig, but that it was such a surprise. . . . I believe it's our job to convince Anya that she can feel safe coming back to school, regardless of how many people know about her wig. Perhaps if you all write her a letter apologizing for staring during gym, and promising to be supportive if she returns—and do I have any volunteers to go down to the library to do some research on alopecia areata?"

Mrs. Hobson was reacting like such a teacher, Keely thought. She acted like this was no different from making Tyler write an apology note to the school cook: "I am sorry I burped in your face when you asked me if I wanted cheese or pepperoni pizza. . . ." She acted like this was no different from sending a kid down to the library when someone asked a question Mrs. Hobson herself couldn't answer: "Well, Sammy, I honestly can't say I know whether Jesse Owens could run faster than a cheetah. Why don't you go on down to the library and find out?" This *was* different. This was Anya maybe dying—

Keely remembered that Anya didn't have cancer after all. She wasn't going to die. But she had lost her hair. In her mind's eye Keely could still see how strange Anya had looked standing there without her wig. How naked. How terrified.

Keely raised her hand.

"I'll go to the library," she volunteered.

"Thank you, Keely," Mrs. Hobson said. "Would anybody else like to go with Keely?"

None of the others raised their hand. They looked scared, like they might catch alopecia areata just from typing the words into the computer.

Eighteen

Anya didn't go to school on Thursday. She didn't go to school on Friday. She stayed home and lay in bed, eating chicken noodle soup and butterscotch pudding. Sick food.

Anya didn't wear her wig, either. She kept the Cincinnati Reds cap on her head all the time instead, pulled as far down over her ears as possible.

Mom stayed home with Anya. Daddy stopped by school and picked up Anya's books and homework. He brought letters from the rest of her class, too, but she wouldn't look at those. At least the homework gave her something to do. She didn't want to watch TV, because everyone on TV had hair. She didn't want to read, because she was so sick of Camelot she thought it might make her throw up just to open the book. She didn't want to play any games, because then Mom would be there, hovering, starting sentences she could never finish.

"Would . . ."

"Don't you . . ."

"If . . ."

Instead Anya worked alone. She took extra time on all the schoolwork, writing her social studies answers in her best cursive and making little curlicues on all the numbers on the multiplication sheets. As far as she was concerned, she could study at home forever, or until her hair grew back, whichever came first. The rest of her class would probably forget what she looked like. But Mrs. Hobson would remember Anya as the kid with the most beautiful handwriting anyone had ever seen.

Friday night Daddy came in and sat on the edge of Anya's bed.

"What are we going to do, Anya?" he asked quietly.

Anya didn't answer. After a moment she couldn't even see his face. There were too many tears between them— tears in her eyes, tears in his.

Nineteen

"**K**eely—wait!"

It was Stef. Keely kept walking. She walked faster, in fact, racing out to second recess with the pack of other kids.

Keely had been avoiding Stef for two days. She couldn't believe she'd ever wanted to be friends with someone who'd do what Stef had done. The first couple of recesses she hadn't known what to do or where to go, but she'd fallen in with Fumi and Yolanda after she saw them drawing on the chalkboard. They were nice. She liked them. They liked her. They liked art every bit as much as she did. She couldn't believe she'd never paid much attention to either of them before.

Then something strange had happened at the start of the first recess on Friday. Nicole and Tory had come over to the table where Yolanda was showing Fumi and Keely how to make braided necklaces.

"Can we try that too?" Nicole had asked.

Yolanda had silently handed over the lengths of string.

Keely had wondered what Stef was doing at recess without any of her friends, but Keely hadn't asked. She didn't want anyone to think that she cared.

Now it was recess again, and Stef was screaming at her.

"Keely, I mean it! Stop right now!"

Keely turned around long enough to say, "You're not my boss. Leave me alone."

It felt so good to say those words. Keely felt like they'd been building up inside her for nearly five years.

"No, please, just listen," Stef begged. "I mean, I know I'm not your boss. You don't have to do anything I say. But I was just hoping . . ."

Were those tears in Stef's eyes? Stef never cried. Stef never begged. She never just hoped. She bulldozed people, she took no prisoners, she walked all over everyone else to get what she wanted. Stef was so horrible she would even rip a wig off the head of a girl she thought was dying of cancer.

Keely stopped. She leaned back against the wall and narrowed her eyes at Stef.

"What do you want?" she asked.

"Everybody's mad at me," Stef said. "Tory, Nicole, you—everyone. They all think I pulled Anya's wig off that day in the gym. Mrs. Vance and Mrs. Hobson even sent me down to the principal's office because of the rumors going around. But I didn't do it, Keely, I swear I didn't. Everyone says you were the one who saw me—you have to tell people that's just not true."

Old habits almost made Keely agree instantly: "Okay, Stef, whatever you say." And then she should cower and beg for forgiveness. But Stef was cowering and begging. Somehow Keely was the one with power now.

"How do I know it's not true?" she asked.

"Did you see me do anything to Anya?"

"No," Keely admitted. "But you wanted Tory or Nicole or me to pull on her wig. I just thought you'd decided to do it yourself."

"But I didn't. I wouldn't have pulled it all the way off. Not in front of everybody. Keely, you have to believe me!"

"You were laughing," Keely said. "I saw you, afterward. You had your hand over your mouth and you were laughing."

"I wasn't! Oh, never mind!" Stef whirled around and ran away—not toward the playground with all the other kids, but back toward the building. Keely stood still and watched her friend—her former friend—speed away in a cloud of red hair.

What if Stef was telling the truth?

In her mind Keely replayed what she'd seen that day in the gym. Anya without her wig, Stef behind her with her hand over her mouth . . . Stef might not have been laughing. She might just have been gasping. She might have been every bit as stunned and horrified as everybody else.

"Oh, no," Keely breathed.

What did Anya think?

Twenty

"**Y**ou want me to drive you where?" Mom asked Saturday morning as she whizzed through the living room straightening crooked pillows.

"To Anya Seaver's house. She's a girl in my class. I looked up the address. It's not very far," Keely said.

"Anya Seaver?" Mom pulled a dead leaf from a houseplant. "Isn't that the girl Stef was trying to make you think had cancer?"

That was how it went with Mom. Just when Keely decided Mom was too busy to pay attention to a single word Keely said, Mom would remember the wrong thing.

"She doesn't have cancer," Keely said. "She's got alope- cia areata. It's a disease that makes people's hair fall out. That's why she was wearing the wig. But she's perfectly healthy otherwise."

Mom gave Keely a measuring look.

"This isn't some dare of Stef's, is it?"

"No, Mom," Keely said. "This is entirely my own idea."

Mom raised one eyebrow and cocked her head thoughtfully. But a moment later she was busy doing something else: sorting the *Newsweek*s from the *House Beautiful*s in the magazine rack.

"Jacob's got a birthday party to go to at eleven, at Chuck E. Cheese," Mom said without even looking up. "If it's on the way, I can drop you off at this Anya's then. You're sure it's all right with her parents?"

Keely couldn't bear the thought of calling Anya's par- ents, explaining, asking permission. It was going to take all the nerve she had just to go talk to Anya. Keely had made a deal with herself: If she knocked on Anya's door and some- one answered and said she could come in, she'd talk to Anya. But if nobody answered or if Anya's mom or dad said, "Sorry, Anya doesn't want visitors right now," then it would mean that Keely wasn't supposed to tell Anya anything, it was none of Keely's business, just like Mom had said way back at the beginning of the week.

"Just give me a ride. I'll take care of everything else," Keely said.

So at eleven fifteen, after Mom and Keely had left Jacob

with a horde of screaming five-year-olds at Chuck E. Cheese, Mom drove down a quiet street full of older, well-kept houses.

"It's number 347," Keely said. "Right there."

"So they'll be dropping you off afterward?" Mom said.

Keely hadn't even thought of that problem.

"Or I'll call," Keely said. Maybe she'd just have to walk home by herself. She'd never done anything like that before.

She stepped out of the SUV, and it seemed like an even greater distance than ever down to the ground. She pushed open a wooden gate and walked slowly up the sidewalk. She felt every bit as intrepid as all those explorers they studied at school, sailing off into unknown waters. She rang the doorbell, and the door opened. Behind her she heard Mom drive off, and she felt abandoned. But why shouldn't Mom drive away? She thought Keely was expected, welcome.

"Yes?"

A woman stood in the doorway regarding Keely. Anya's mom. Keely gulped.

"Hi. I'm Keely Michaels. From Anya's class at school. I, um, need to tell her something that might make her feel better about coming back to school."

Anya's mother pushed the door open wider, letting Keely in. Keely looked around a small, cozy living room. "Is Anya here?"

"She's in her room. She's been a little . . . upset. Just a minute." The woman turned and hollered down a hallway. "Todd?"

A man came out from the hall. Keely guessed it was Anya's dad.

"Todd, this is one of Anya's friends from school. She wanted to tell Anya something that she thinks will help her. Do you think—"

"Why not?" Anya's dad said. "It's worth a try." He didn't sound very sure of himself.

"Go on down the hall, honey," Anya's mom said. "It's the first door on the right."

"Shouldn't you tell her I'm here, ask her if . . ."

Anya's mom winced.

"She's more likely to let you in if we don't ask," she said.

Both of Anya's parents stepped aside, letting Keely past. Keely was surprised by how easily they faded into the background. They seemed as insubstantial as ghosts, compared with her own parents. If Keely had been the one who'd lost her hair, Keely's dad would be standing right outside her bedroom door, not letting anyone see her if she didn't want to be seen. And Keely's mom—well, Keely was almost certain her mother would turn the whole world upside down finding a cure. No—she'd probably invent one herself.

Keely had never before loved her parents quite so much as she did, right then, watching Anya's.

Keely walked down the hall and knocked on the first door she came to. Nobody answered, but emboldened, Keely shoved the door open and walked in.

Twenty-One

Anya didn't even bother turning her head when she heard the door open. Was it lunchtime already? She'd have to muster the energy to tell Mom she wasn't hungry.

"Anya?" a voice said, and it wasn't Mom or Dad. It was Keely Michaels.

For one awful instant Anya thought someone had cooked up a scheme to bring the whole school to her, since she wouldn't go to school. But it was just Keely, standing there alone. All the same, Anya pulled her cap down as far as she could.

"Anya, hi. I hope I'm not bothering you. Your mom and dad said it was okay to come in. I just wanted to tell you . . ."

Keely seemed to be having trouble figuring out what to say next.

"What?" Anya said.

"I just wanted to tell you, well, I was afraid that you thought that Stef pulled off your wig on purpose. I thought she did too, because, well, you know Stef. You know how she gets. But she swore to me that she had nothing to do with your wig coming off. It must have gotten caught on the Velcro on the mats or something. Or maybe someone just stepped on it by accident and didn't know. So if that's the reason you haven't wanted to come back to school, because you're afraid people will be pulling your wig off left and right, well, you don't have to worry about that at all. You can come back to school and nobody will bother you."

Keely made that whole speech without taking a single breath. When she stopped, the room seemed more silent than ever.

Anya blinked. She had never really thought about *how* her wig had come off. For three days she'd been trying to forget that it ever had.

"You thought everything was Stef's fault?" she asked slowly.

"Well, yeah. Just because Stef noticed that you were wearing a wig, and she was really curious about it, and she wanted Tory or Nicole or me to tug on it, just a little, to see if it really was a wig—I mean, not hard enough to hurt you, of course. But—"

"Why didn't you tell me you knew?" Anya interrupted.

"We didn't want to be *rude*," Keely said.

Anya suddenly saw how it must have been: Every single kid in her class—maybe even every single kid in the school—had known all along that she'd been wearing a wig. They'd probably been laughing at her behind her back from the very beginning. They'd probably even been laughing at her before the wig, back when she got her first few bald patches.

Anya felt her face go hot with shame.

"And we thought you might have cancer," Keely continued. "We'd never heard of alopecia areata. So we thought you might be dying. And we didn't know how to talk to someone who was dying."

Anya remembered the rushed way Keely had spoken to her that one day at recess, when Anya had been terrified Keely would notice the wig. Keely had already known.

"How do you know how to talk to someone with alopecia areata?" Anya challenged.

Now it was Keely's turn to turn red. She stared down at her shoes.

"I don't," she said. "I just wanted to make you feel better. I just thought—well, I don't know, I was blaming Stef, and I thought you might too."

Anya didn't say anything right away. She'd been alone so much the past few days, it was kind of bewildering to try to carry on a conversation.

"Keely," she finally said. "I never thought about it being Stef's fault that my wig came off."

"Then, why don't you come back to school?"

Anya stared at Keely. Innocent, ignorant Keely with all that long brown hair.

"Didn't you see me?" Anya practically whimpered. "Without my wig? Everyone saw. How can I ever go back—"

"But, Anya," Keely said. "You were beautiful. I mean— this is the other thing I wanted to tell you. Maybe you felt weird because you don't have hair—I guess I'd feel weird about it too. But when I saw you without your wig, it was like you were the prettiest girl in the class. You didn't look ordinary, like the rest of us. You looked like a movie star or a singer, someone who looks really different from everyone else. Different good, I mean, not different bad."

Keely was one of those kids who never said much at school. Like Anya herself. But whenever Keely spoke— even if it was just something like answering a math question—she always looked over at Stef, like she had to make sure Stef approved. Anya was so stunned by this sudden torrent of chatter from Keely that she could barely make sense of what Keely was saying.

Then the words sank in.

Beautiful? Keely thought I looked beautiful without my wig?

A harsh laugh escaped from Anya's throat. Or maybe it wasn't a laugh. Maybe she was crying again.

"Keely," she said. "I lost my hair. It just fell out, for no reason. And now I'm scared to go back to school because I know everyone will make fun of me. Or, even if they don't do that, they'll *stare*. They'll talk about me behind my back. They'll be scared that being around me might make their hair fall out too.

"And at night I can hear my parents crying because they don't know what to do, because they can't fix what's wrong with me, because . . ." She couldn't choke out the rest of her words. *Because they wish they had a daughter with hair. Because now they're scared to have another child, because that one might not have hair either. Because they're ashamed of me.*

"Crying?" Keely said. "Even your dad?"

"Even my dad," Anya said. "Have you ever seen your dad cry?"

Silently Keely shook her head no.

"And now you're telling me you thought I looked beautiful? Is that supposed to make me feel good?"

Keely shrugged. "I'm sorry," she whispered. "Can't . . . can't I do anything to help?"

Anya stared at Keely. Keely had been in the same class as Anya since kindergarten. Keely had learned to read the same time as Anya, had learned her multiplication tables the same time as Anya. Keely brought in chocolate-iced cupcakes every year on her birthday, just like Anya did. But Keely also had long, thick brown hair flowing halfway down her back, and Anya didn't.

Anya turned her face toward the wall.

"You can't help," she said. "Not unless you want to give me your hair."

Twenty-Two

Keely stumbled out of Anya's room and back into the Seavers' living room. Keely was almost surprised to see bright sunlight streaming in the living-room windows. She felt like she'd been in Anya's room so long it should be night by now. *Days* should have passed.

Anya's parents were standing there, waiting. They rushed toward Keely.

"Did you . . ."

"Were you able . . ."

Keely looked from Anya's mother to her father and back again. She remembered what Anya had said about hearing her parents crying at night. They looked like such nice, ordinary people—both of them in jeans and sweatshirts, the same kind of clothes Keely's parents wore on the weekend. But their faces were taken over with worry. Anya's mom was wringing her hands; Anya's dad had his fists clenched.

Keely suddenly wondered if her own parents would be as strong and invincible as she'd thought if she ever got something like alopecia areata. Maybe she'd want them to cry, too.

"Anya's still upset," Keely reported. "I . . . I don't think I helped at all."

Anya's last words still echoed in her ears: *"Not unless you want to give me your hair . . . Not unless you want to give me your hair . . ."* Anya had looked so sad saying that. So defeated.

"Oh," Anya's dad said. His shoulders slumped. "Well, thanks for trying."

"We're going to take her to a counselor," Anya's mother confided. "She's not coping very well. And really"—she glanced at her husband—"neither are we."

"You should join a support group," Keely said.

Anya's parents just looked at her. Keely felt weird all of a sudden. She wasn't used to giving grown-ups advice. She scrambled to explain.

"When Mrs. Hobson told our class what was wrong with Anya—that she has alopecia areata, I mean—she made us do some research about the disease. I read all about this group called the National Alopecia Areata Foundation—

National Foundation for Alopecia Areata?—something like that. And they have support groups all over the country for people with alopecia and their families, and a Web site and stuff. I don't know. There were just a bunch of people on the Internet saying it helped to talk to other people who knew what it was like."

"Maybe we should try that," Anya's mom said.

Keely couldn't tell if Anya's mom was serious or if that was just one of those things grown-ups said to kids—"Sure, sure, we'll give it a try." Maybe Mrs. Seaver was even being sarcastic, like Anya. "Not unless you want to give me your hair." It wasn't like Keely could *really* do anything to help Anya and her family.

Or could she?

Suddenly Keely had an idea.

"Is your mom coming back for you?" Anya's dad asked. "Or do you want us to drop you off somewhere?"

Keely looked him straight in the eye.

"I'll walk," she said. "Just let me call home and tell them I'm on my way."

Keely hoped Mom would let her walk by herself. Because Keely had something to think about now, and she wanted to figure everything out before she told anyone else.

She'd remembered something else she'd read on the Internet, and something Tory had said.

Maybe, just maybe, she could give Anya her hair.

Twenty-Three

Anya could hear her parents' muffled voices. They were talking to Keely. Then she heard the front door open and close, which probably meant Keely was leaving. Why did Anya feel disappointed? What had she possibly thought Keely could do for her?

"But, Anya. You were beautiful. . . ."

If Anya had thought about it ahead of time, those would have been the last possible words she would ever have expected Keely to say to her. Beautiful. *Beautiful.* Stef Englewood was beautiful, with all that wavy red hair swirling around her face. Nicole, one of Keely's other friends, always looked pretty great too because she had long blond hair that curled up at the ends. Or, no, you couldn't really say she was beautiful, because she had kind of a crooked nose and her eyes were a little too close together. She just had beautiful hair.

Could someone be beautiful with ugly hair? Or—no hair?

Anya sat up straight. She eased her legs out of bed and walked, very slowly, over to her dresser. Her dresser with the mirror. The wig stand and the wig weren't there anymore; Mom and Dad hadn't put them back after Anya threw them out in the hall. So there was nothing between Anya and the mirror she'd barely glanced in since November.

Really she hadn't glanced in it much before that either. Anya had never been someone who cared much about how she looked. Not before, anyway.

And since—since she lost her hair—she'd looked in the mirror only when she had her wig on, or when she had the cap pulled down so far over her ears that no one could ever have known what was underneath.

But now she stood squarely in front of the mirror. She grasped the bill of her cap and lifted it a centimeter, an inch—all the way off. And still she kept her eyes trained on the mirror, staring into the eyes of her own reflection. And then she looked above her reflected eyes to where she'd once had hair.

She was bald. Completely bald.

She'd kind of suspected that before. In the rare moments she'd been without the cap or the wig, she'd felt no tickle of hair against her head in a long time. She'd seen so much hair come out—on her pillow, on the carpet, in the shower—she would have been surprised to have any left. And Mom, attaching the wig with the toupee tape so precisely every morning, had never once moaned, "Oh, this is going to pull out what little hair you have left. . . ."

But Anya had been very careful never actually to touch her hairless scalp; she'd been very careful never to look and see what everyone else had seen in gym class.

She looked now. She reached up her hand and touched her bare skin, almost stroking it, not quite daring to think about how it felt.

She was bald. Completely bald.

No matter how long she'd suspected that, no matter how long she'd known, it was still a jolt to see her familiar face without any hair above it, not even the wig. It was like looking at one of those trick photos—an ordinary face on an alien's head. Or like a Halloween costume—"*Amazing*," people might say, "*it looks so real.*"

It wasn't a costume. It wasn't a trick. She really was bald.

Keely's words teased at her again: "*Beautiful . . . You were beautiful. . . .*" Was that true?

For a second Anya could almost see it. Without the distraction of hair, her eyes looked bigger, her nose straighter, her mouth redder. If she still had hair, if she'd never heard of alopecia areata and she'd been flipping through one of her mom's magazines and seen a picture that looked like she looked now in the mirror, the word *beautiful* might have flickered in her mind.

But so would *strange*. So would *weird*. So would *what's wrong with her?*

Twenty-Four

How did Stef do it? How did she get other people to do what she wanted them to?

Keely had a plan now, but it depended on convincing her friends to do something they probably wouldn't like. In her head everything made sense, but the plan started going shaky the minute she opened her mouth and started explaining to someone else. To Mom.

"Oh, honey, are you sure?" Mom asked. "Are you sure it would do Anya any good? This isn't something you can change your mind about. Especially not if you talk any of the other girls into going along with you."

"I'm sure," Keely said in a voice that sounded anything but.

They were talking in the kitchen while Mom washed dishes. Mom had let Keely walk home by herself—miracle number one. And now Mom was listening closely and nodding and shaking her head and answering and never once changing the subject or saying she didn't have time or commanding, "Go get ready for . . . ," or, "Go do your homework." That was miracle number two. Keely just needed a few more miracles.

"Well, it's up to you," Mom said, putting the last dish in the drainer and rinsing out the sink. "I think you're old enough to make a decision like this on your own."

Hearing Mom say that, Keely felt thrilled and scared, all at once.

She sat down with the cordless phone and two lists. One had the names of girls in her class with long hair. The other was the list of girls with short hair. She started with the second list first. All she wanted from them was a promise.

An hour later Mom walked through the family room with an overflowing laundry basket balanced on her hip. By then Keely had dropped the phone on the floor and crumpled both lists.

"How'd you do?" Mom asked.

"The best answers I got were 'I'll think about it' and 'I'll let you know later,'" Keely said in a muffled voice. "Nobody said yes."

Mom sat down on the couch.

"It is a lot to ask," she said gently. "You can't blame the other kids for wanting to think about it."

"That's just an excuse," Keely said sulkily. "None of them are going to do it."

"So, what are you going to do?" Mom asked. "You don't always have to do things in a group, you know. Is this important enough that you'll do it alone?"

Keely wanted to squirm away from Mom's gaze. She thought about Anya sitting in her dark room all by herself, not even able to be comforted by her mom and dad. She thought about how Anya had looked that day in gym, so frightened and alone, even though she was surrounded by other kids.

"Yeah," she said. "This is important enough that I want to do it alone."

Mom looked straight at Keely for a long time. She didn't reach for the laundry at her feet; she didn't slide forward on the couch to prepare for standing up and walking away. She just stared into Keely's eyes. And then she said something she'd never said to Keely before in Keely's entire life.

"Keely, I am so proud of you."

Twenty-Five

Keely was coming back to Anya's. It was weird. Before today Keely had never been to Anya's house even once in the entire five years they'd known each other. And now she was about to make her second visit in a single day.

"Why?" Anya said when Mom hung up the phone and told her.

"She says she has a surprise for you," Mom said.

"Oh," Anya said. Any other time she might have asked for details, might even have called up Keely herself and demanded to know what was going on. But Anya was still feeling shaky from staring at her bald head in the mirror for so long. And she'd actually forced herself to leave her room. She'd had lunch with Mom and Dad in the kitchen, and now she was playing solitaire on the living-room floor.

"When's she coming?" Anya asked, laying a red two on a black three.

"In about an hour," Mom said. "Do you . . . do you want to put your wig on first?"

Anya turned over three more cards while she considered the question.

"No," she finally decided. "She's seen me without a wig before. The cap's good enough. I don't think Keely cares."

It was strange to say that. Anya wondered if it was true. What if nobody else in her class cared either? What if she went back to school and didn't bother wearing a wig or a cap, just went as she naturally was?

Anya couldn't quite get her mind around that possibility. She felt odd even thinking about it. But everyone had seen her bald head already. She couldn't pretend anymore that she still had hair.

An hour later Anya was standing before her bedroom mirror again, trying to figure out the best angle for her cap. Too far backward, and the cap revealed that she didn't have any hair at the front of her head. Too far forward, and it showed the vast emptiness at the back. Anya was about to give up and beg Mom to hurry up and put the wig on, when she heard the doorbell. She rushed over and turned her light out. She made sure the shade was pulled as far down over the window as possible. But that didn't help. It had gotten so sunny this afternoon that Anya's room was still quite bright.

Anya thought about going to the living room and talking to Keely out there. She *was* curious about Keely's surprise. But it was even brighter out there. Out there Keely would be able to see every single empty hair follicle.

Anya leaned back against her bed and waited. It took a long time. Had Keely come to see Anya, or just Anya's parents?

Anya had just about decided to give in to her curiosity and walk on out to the living room, when someone tapped on the door.

"Anya?" Keely called. "Can I come in?"

Anya opened the door.

At first she almost didn't recognize Keely. She'd never seen Keely without long hair before; even when they were in kindergarten, Keely's hair had reached halfway down her back. But now Keely's hair was chopped even with the bottom of her ears. It made her look different. Older, maybe. More grown up.

Anya was so busy staring at Keely's hair that she didn't notice what Keely held in her hands until Keely lifted it up, level with Anya's eyes.

It was Anya's wig stand. But someone—Keely?—had drawn eyes and a mouth and a nose on it. It didn't look blank and anonymous anymore. It looked like Anya.

And instead of holding a wig on top, the wig stand was covered with one thick braid of hair that stretched from one side to the other, tied at both ends and dangling over the ears. The braid was the same color as Keely's hair. Could it be . . . ?

"You said I couldn't help unless I gave you my hair," Keely said simply. "So I did."

Anya didn't know what to say.

"How . . . ?"

"I read some stuff on the Internet," Keely said. "About alopecia areata. And one of the things it said was that wigs made from real hair are much better than fake ones, than synthetic hair. They fit better, with something called a vacuum seal, so they don't come off. And they look better too. Nobody would know the difference.

"But the real-hair wigs are more expensive and they're harder to get because, well, it's not like there's a bunch of hair lying around that wig makers can use. But there are ways for people to donate their hair, to make wigs for kids. So that's what I did. For you. I'm giving you my hair. We're going to send it away and it'll come back as a wig you can wear that won't ever fall off."

She held the wig stand out even closer to Anya, almost like she expected Anya to pick up the braid and glue it on her head right then and there.

Anya started crying. She didn't really know why. She could see Mom and Dad hovering behind Keely in the hall, watching her reaction. And behind them she could see another woman she guessed was Keely's mom, watching too. Everyone was waiting to see what Anya would say.

"It's . . . ," Anya began. She gulped. "It's not enough."

She saw Keely's face fall. Now Keely looked like she was going to cry too. "Oh, Keely, I'm sorry. It's—I mean, this was really nice of you. To try. And to cut your hair—you had so much hair. It's just, even with this, even with you giving me your hair, even with the best wig in the world, I still have alopecia areata. I'm still bald. I'll still have to wear a wig anytime I want to look normal."

Keely sniffled.

"I wanted the other girls in the class to donate their hair too," Keely said. "It takes a lot of hair to make a wig. And the ones with short hair, I wanted them to promise to grow their hair out and donate it too. For other kids with alopecia. I wanted you to know—well, it's not just the hair. It's not just a wig I wanted to give you. I wanted to show you we cared. I called them all. But I'm not good at convincing people to do things. They're all still thinking about it."

Anya tried to imagine timid, mousy Keely trying to convince anyone of anything. She thought of Keely calling all the other girls. She wouldn't have thought Keely would be brave enough even to dial the numbers. But she had been. She'd been brave enough to come and talk to Anya, too, and no one else had done that. And she'd offered Anya her hair.

"Why?" Anya asked, suddenly bewildered. "Why would you do all this for me?"

Keely looked down at the floor. "When we thought you were dying of cancer," she began, "Stef kept saying, 'We've got to think of a way to help.' But we didn't do anything because we didn't know what to do. And we were kind of freaked out. I mean, someone our age—dying? And then when we found out you didn't have cancer, you had alopecia areata instead, it made me think. You'd looked like you felt like you were dying. You looked that sad.

"And I thought, maybe, in a way, it might feel as bad to keep living with something like alopecia areata as it does dying of cancer. I mean, if you die—you die, that's it. Maybe you even go to heaven, and everything's better then. But if you keep living, feeling miserable every day, you've got to keep getting up every day, facing your problems every day. So when I thought there was something I could do to change that for you, I had to try. You know?"

Keely understands, Anya thought. *She understands why it was so wrong of the doctor to say, "At least she doesn't have cancer." She understands that it's not just hair that I lost. She understands why I've been lying in bed for three days.*

"I wasn't really facing anything," Anya admitted. "I've really just been hiding."

She reached out, made herself pick up the thick braid of hair draped over the wig stand. It was kind of gross, touching someone else's cut-off hair. But she didn't let herself shiver. She reminded herself that Keely was sharing. This wasn't Keely's hair anymore. It was hers.

"Thank you," Anya said.

Twenty-Six

Anya's seat was still empty Monday morning.

As she slid into her own chair Keely felt a little jolt of disappointment. All that she'd done—all that she'd tried to do—had been for nothing. She missed her hair. It was weird to be able to feel the air on the back of her neck. She kept automatically tossing her head, like she always did to flip her hair over her shoulder. Except she didn't have enough hair anymore to flip.

She was sure everyone was staring at her, whispering behind her back.

Like they'd done with Anya.

"Good morning, class," Mrs. Hobson said. "I have some

good news for you. Anya will be returning today. She has a doctor's appointment this morning, but she'll be back this afternoon. While she's away, I would like to remind all of you about behaving appropriately around her. I'm sure I can count on all of you not to ask rude questions, not to make cruel comments, not to act like anything's different at all."

Someone was slipping something into Keely's hand. Keely felt the brush of fingertips and was left clutching a piece of paper folded over many times. Keeping her eyes trained on Mrs. Hobson, she unfurled the paper under the desk. When it was flat, she casually slid the paper onto the desktop and glanced down.

LOOK AT STEF!!!!! the note said.

Keely turned her head. She'd been so focused on Anya's empty chair, she hadn't really looked at anyone else in the whole classroom. But there was Nicole, two rows away, motioning with her head and rolling her eyes. Keely looked beyond, at Stef.

Stef had short hair now. It was the same length as Keely's.

Stef pointed and grinned, and mouthed words even Keely could understand: "I donated mine, too!"

Stef had never said she was going to do that.

Confused, Keely glanced back at the note on her desk. Under LOOK AT STEF!!!!! it said, SHE IS SUCH A COPYCAT!

And Keely understood that people were still mad at Stef.

Keely herself wondered if Stef had donated her hair just to try to get everyone to like her again, not because she really cared about Anya.

Did it matter? Regardless of why Stef had done it, some kid somewhere in the world was going to get a curly red wig because of Stef.

Keely raised her hand.

"But Mrs. Hobson, something is different," she said. "Anya lost her hair and now she has to wear a wig. And everyone saw her and she ran away. And Stef and I both donated our hair to help kids like Anya, with alopecia areata, or even kids with cancer. And some other girls are thinking about doing that too. Lots of things have changed."

Keely knew she wasn't saying what she wanted to say. She wanted to tell everyone that Anya losing her hair had been really good for her, Keely, because it had made her brave, and it had made her think for herself and not just follow Stef. But that didn't seem fair to Anya, because nobody could say losing her hair had been good for Anya.

Everyone was staring at Keely anyway. She'd forgotten that she never spoke out in class unless she had to. She'd even forgotten to wait for Mrs. Hobson to call on her.

"Okay," Mrs. Hobson said slowly. "I see your point. How do *you* think we should behave, Keely?"

"I think we should ask Anya," Keely said.

Twenty-Seven

Mom pulled up in front of the school.

"Do you want me to come in with you?" she asked.

Slowly Anya shook her head. "It's just school," she said.

She opened her door but didn't get out right away. She turned back to face Mom.

"Mom, this is a bad day, right?"

"Well . . . ," Mom said. "You got out of school for a half day, and I took you to Wendy's for lunch. So if you look on the bright side—"

"No," Anya said. "I don't want to look on the bright side right now. It's a bad day. The doctor said the new treatment might not work any better than the last one did.

And now I've got to go into school, where everyone's going to stare at me because they saw me without my wig last week. So it's a bad day."

Mom started to protest, but Anya wouldn't let her interrupt.

"And I just wanted to say, even on a bad day like today, I still think that you and Dad should have another baby. Even if the baby has alopecia areata, too."

Mom's jaw dropped. "What? Who told you we were—"

"I heard," Anya said. "I'm sorry. I didn't mean to eavesdrop."

Mom seemed to be thinking. "Did you hear anything else?"

"Yeah," Anya said. "You're worried about me swimming and going to sleepovers and getting dates when I'm in high school. You cry about that."

Mom frowned apologetically.

"You're my little girl," Mom said. "I just want to protect you—"

"But you can't," Anya said. "This is making me grow up. So I think you should have a new baby if you want someone to protect."

Mom just stared at Anya. Then she smiled a little ruefully. She had tears in her eyes, but they didn't escape and roll down her cheeks.

"All right. I'll talk this over with Dad again. I'm glad . . ." She swallowed hard. "I'm glad you feel this way." Very carefully she brushed aside the bangs of Anya's wig and kissed her on the forehead. "You are growing up," she said. "With or without hair."

Anya nodded and eased out of the car. She signed in at the office and began walking down the long, long hallway to her classroom. Nobody else was out in the hall—there was still time to turn around and run back to Mom. No one would see.

But her legs kept carrying her forward, to Mrs. Hobson's class.

She tried to open the door quietly, but it didn't matter. Everyone turned around and stared. Anya gulped.

"Anya, hello!" Mrs. Hobson said too heartily. "We're so happy to have you back with us."

Nobody looked happy. All the other kids stared in silence, straight at Anya's wig, like they were all trying to develop X-ray vision to see beneath it.

"I have to admit, I've never had a student with alopecia areata before," Mrs. Hobson said. "And we weren't sure whether you'd want to tell us about it, or if you'd rather not even discuss it. Keely suggested that we just ask you, and you can let us know what you prefer. And we will abide by your wishes."

Anya looked at Keely, who gave her a tentative smile.

"*Of course I don't want to talk about it,*" Anya wanted to say. "*I just want it to go away.*"

But it wasn't going away, and she couldn't pretend anymore that no one knew.

"I have alopecia areata," she started. "You all saw what I look like now without a wig."

She looked out at her classmates. Keely and Yolanda and a few others were gazing at her sympathetically. Tyler looked like he was trying not to laugh.

Well, why not let him?

"I know you're all probably jealous because *I* never have to wash my hair now," Anya said. "And my parents never tell me to go brush my hair. In fact, it's better for the wig if I don't brush or comb it much at all. So I have my mom telling me, 'No, no, put that comb down!'"

Tyler laughed first. A little ripple of giggles spread across the room.

"And when summertime comes, if I get hot playing soccer, I'll be able to just take my hair off," Anya continued.

"Oh, man! You're so lucky!" Tyler shouted out.

Anya closed her eyes briefly. *"Summertime?"* Why had she said that? She wouldn't be able to bear it if she still didn't have her hair back by summertime.

No, she could bear it. She might have to.

Anya opened her eyes. For the first time her gaze fell on Stef.

"Oh, my gosh, Stef," she blurted out. "Did you donate your hair too?"

Stef ran her fingers through her now short hair.

"Yes," she said. "Doesn't it look great? I thought this was the least I could do. Alopecia areata's sort of like an allergy, right? I know what that's like. *I* broke out in hives once just from putting glitter gel on my face. I have such sensitive skin. Anyhow, I think every girl in this class should donate her hair too. The ones that can, I mean. It'd be the greatest thing. They'd probably even put an article in the newspaper about us or something."

Anya stifled the urge to giggle. Stef certainly did like to be the center of attention. If there was a newspaper article, she'd probably tell the reporter the whole thing had been her idea. Anya's eyes met Keely's. Keely looked amused too. It was like Anya and Keely were having a secret conversation: *Let her talk. We don't care.*

"All right," Mrs. Hobson said. "It's time for math. We can talk about all this some other time, if Anya wants."

Anya slipped into her seat—a girl with a wig in a classroom full of kids with hair. A girl who would be totally exposed if Stef got her way and there was an article in the newspaper.

But she was also a girl who had friends, including one who'd given up her own hair for Anya. And, Anya reminded herself, she was a girl who might have a new baby brother or sister someday soon.

And maybe, just maybe, she'd get her hair back too . . .

Anya remembered what she'd asked her mother in the car: "This is a bad day, right?" It didn't seem so awful anymore. And, with or without hair, she could imagine better days ahead.

Afterword

Alopecia areata affects more than four million people in the United States. The disease usually begins—as Anya's did—with one or more small, smooth patches on the scalp. Some people lose only small amounts of hair and regrow it within a year. Others may lose all the hair on their scalp (this is called alopecia totalis) or on their entire body (alopecia universalis).

Although alopecia areata affects people of all ages, the disease generally begins in childhood. There is no cure; medical treatments may or may not help. And the hair that does grow back may fall out again, sometimes repeatedly over the course of many years. People with alopecia areata

say that's one of the hardest parts of having the disease—
never knowing when or if they'll have hair.

If you want to help kids with alopecia areata, you can—
just like Keely did. A group called Locks of Love accepts
donations of hair to make wigs for financially disadvan-
taged kids who have lost their own hair because of alopecia
areata or other medical problems. More than 80 percent of
the people who donate hair to Locks of Love are kids
themselves.

Locks of Love requires that donated hair be at least ten
inches long, clean, dry, and bundled in a ponytail or braid.
For more details, contact Locks of Love, 1640 South
Congress Avenue, Suite 104, Palm Springs, Florida 33461,
or visit their Web site, *www.locksoflove.org*.

For more information about alopecia areata, contact the
National Alopecia Areata Foundation, P.O. Box 150760,
San Rafael, California 94915-0760, or visit their Web site,
www.alopeciaareata.com. Another helpful website, designed
as an online forum with lots of links, is *www.alopeciakids.org*.

MARGARET PETERSON HADDIX is the best-selling author of many books for children and teens. Her books for young readers include *Running Out of Time*, *Among the Hidden*, *Among the Impostors*, *Among the Betrayed*, and *The Girl with 500 Middle Names*. Her work has been honored with the International Reading Association Children's Book Award, American Library Association Best Book for Young Adults and Quick Pick for Reluctant Young Adult Readers citations, and several state Readers' Choice Awards. Margaret Peterson Haddix lives with her family in Columbus, Ohio.